Rufus Ellis

A Sermon Occasioned by the Death of William Hickling Prescott

Anatiposi

Rufus Ellis

A Sermon Occasioned by the Death of William Hickling Prescott

Reprint of the original, first published in 1859.

1st Edition 2023 | ISBN: 978-3-38231-296-1

Anatiposi Verlag is an imprint of Outlook Verlagsgesellschaft mbH.

Verlag (Publisher): Outlook Verlag GmbH, Zeilweg 44, 60439 Frankfurt, Deutschland
Vertretungsberechtigt (Authorized to represent): E. Roepke, Zeilweg 44, 60439 Frankfurt, Deutschland
Druck (Print): Books on Demand GmbH, In de Tarpen 42, 22848 Norderstedt, Deutschland

The Joy of the Christian Mourner:

A

SERMON

Occasioned by the Death

OF

WILLIAM HICKLING PRESCOTT,

PREACHED IN THE FIRST CHURCH,

FEB. 6, 1859.

———

BY RUFUS ELLIS.

———

PUBLISHED BY THE REQUEST OF THE SOCIETY.

BOSTON:

CROSBY, NICHOLS, AND COMPANY,

117, WASHINGTON STREET.

1859.

SERMON.

John xiv. 28: "If ye loved me, ye would rejoice, because I said, I go unto the Father."

LET us admit, at the outset, that it is a very high strain. The words must have seemed, at first, a very hard saying to the disciples: they may seem so to us. Those disciples did love their Lord, and yet hardly in that wise. They did love their Lord; but their hearts were troubled when they heard him speak of going away. Nevertheless, the time came when his joy was fulfilled in them; when the invisible Lord of glory, restored at once to the bosom of the Father and to the communion of his believing children, was more to them even than the dear friend, the sweet light of whose heavenly face had made their world so bright and beautiful. The strain, I say, is a high one. The joy of which the Saviour speaks may be thought to be beyond our measure. The words, though caught from the most loving lips that ever framed themselves to human speech, may even sound strange and harsh; and yet, as is ever found to be the case with the hard sayings of the gospel, we have here a great affirmation of a transcendent faith, a portion of absolute truth which is sure to be accepted, sooner or later, by all who are of the truth.

The joy of which our Saviour speaks supposes a very elevated and pure affection, — an affection far transcending in quality and measure the love with which too many of us love one another; and it supposes also a great faith, — a soul that has felt the powers, and is persuaded of the realities, of the world to come. Such joy and such faith may well be numbered amongst the highest Christian attainments, to be made our own only in proportion as we exercise ourselves in the discipline of the Master, and strive and pray for larger measures of his spirit. We are accustomed to speak of the great duties and the great sacrifices which are proposed for the believer, the exceeding righteousness which should mark the Christian; and they say well who so speak: but great persuasions, great affections, and great joys, as well as great works, are included amongst gospel successes, and go largely to make up our ideal of the Christian character. It is much to do justly and love mercy, by the grace of Christ helping our infirmity: but it is not enough, and we have not had our full portion of the unspeakable gift, unless the gospel has been made to us a source of faith and hope and joy, a sweet fountain of love ; unless it has called up in our hearts a feeling of gladness, nourished by the clear and strong persuasion, that what we cannot see is infinitely more real and glorious than what we can see. *"He that followeth me,"* said the Saviour, *" shall not walk in darkness, but shall have the light of life."* We do not follow Christ with the best and truest following, unless we walk in that light, with a measure of that gladness and single-ness of heart which marked his chosen and nearest disciples, even in the time of their bereavement, as they went from house to house through the streets of that Jerusalem which should know him no more for ever. Let me dwell a moment upon the great thought of our Lord.

1. *" If ye loved me."* The Master supposes an affec-tion so deep, so high, so unselfish, as to rise above the natural desire for the visible presence of the beloved object, — a love so disinterested, that it can rejoice even in a separation, when this separation is mani-festly for the good of our friend. It is not that we do not crave the dear, familiar presence : it is that we will not suffer this craving to prevail over our sense of satisfaction, when we think of the inheritance of light and freedom upon which they enter who die in the Lord. And it is the very quality of love to postpone self, and live only in its object ; to suffer

gladly; yes, to rejoice in the hour of agony, when he
for whom our tears are flowing has gone forward and
upward in going away from us. The wisest human
interpreter of man's heart has expressed this thought
in this wise : —

> " Nay, if you read this line, remember not
> The hand that writ it; for I love you so,
> That I in your sweet thoughts would be forgot,
> If thinking on me then should make you woe.
> Oh! if, I say, you look upon this verse,
> When I perhaps compounded am with clay,
> Do not so much as my poor name rehearse,
> But let your love e'en with my life decay.

So love casts self behind. So love hates and de-
stroys self. Its utmost desire, its great and final
labor, is to fill that other cup of life to overflowing;
and, though separation be only a death in life, it will
take up even that cross, if so its dearer self may be
the gainer.

2. I say, " may be the gainer." We cannot rejoice,
we cannot even be content, in the time of bereavement, unless we are persuaded of this. The disciples
were to be glad, because their Lord was to go to the
Father; because the day of his voluntary humiliation
was soon to come to an end, and he who had gone
about amongst men in the form of a servant, not
eagerly insisting upon his greatness, but drinking to
the dregs the cup of human sorrow, would soon leave
the world, and resume the glory which he had with his

Father before the world was. Blessed and beneficent
as his earthly life had been, that exaltation to the
right hand of God promised a joy and a service far
more glorious. When they were made to realize
this truth, they did rejoice. The light of hope came
again into their eyes, when their steadfast gaze fol-
lowed into the heavens his vanishing form, and his
spirit returned to guide and comfort them, and they
were enabled to do greater works than ever before,
because of the power and the glory which proceeded
from the Father and the Son. It was expedient for
them that he should go away. They lost the limited
humanity; but they were brought nearer to the illi-
mitable divinity, — to the spirit of an everlasting life.
You may say that it was not faith, but knowledge,
that changed the sadness of the disciples into joy.
You may tell me of the evidence afforded to doubting
Thomas, but not afforded to us. You may remind
me that those were days of open vision. But bear in
mind, that, if they saw, it was that they and we might
believe. And consider the words of the Lord to
Thomas: "Thomas, because thou hast seen, thou hast
believed : blessed are they who have not seen, and
yet have believed." There is a Christian persuasion
of the life to come, — a persuasion wrought into the
soul by the words and the wonders of the Saviour's
ministry, by the whole mysterious influence of his

being, — which changes what for so many is only a great darkness into the splendors of the eternal day. If we would rejoice, we must believe, and believe greatly. Nothing but faith and hope can save us from desolation. It is not enough to have risen above those plaintive wailings in which the patient sufferer of the Old Testament breathes out his soul's grief and despair, asking so piteously, " If a man die, shall he live again ? " and getting no answer save this, " There is hope for a tree, if it be cut down, that it will sprout again, and that its tender branches will not fail. . . . But man dieth, and he is gone for ever ! Man expireth, and where is he ? " No answer, — only another question. It is not enough to believe in shadows and spectres, in a land where the light itself is little better than darkness, and thin, airy forms flit about in the distance, and vanish into the gloomy spaces. Speaking of such a heaven as that, the shade of the great Grecian hero might well declare, that he would rather be the slave of the meanest of earth's children, and dwell in the light of day, than reign as king in Hades. We must believe great things concerning the life to come. Not that we can have definite and tangible statement, any more than the blind can have knowledge of colors.

> " What is the heaven our God bestows?
> No prophet yet nor angel knows."

And yet, because the future so surpasses our conceptions, let us not make it shadowy and unreal, or magnify the life to come by putting a slight upon this life. Only by reason of the glory which excelleth shall this world have no glory. Accept the goodness and greatness and beauty of earth; revere and love and cleave to them; and yet believe that they may be transfigured. The Lord was ever majestic and gracious; but how much more so, when, on the mount of vision, the heavenly streamed through the earthly, and his face did shine as the sun, and his raiment was white as the light! Christ has opened the most cheering visions of the light beyond the grave. He hath abolished death. His affirmation of life, — life unceasing, not to be sunk for ages in the slumber of an intermediate state, — life which flows out of time into and through eternity; his affirmation that God is not, and never has been, the God of the dead, but of the living, — is firm and unqualified. It is a life, he says, which we share with himself; for he is that life and that resurrection. We must not fall away from the highest conceptions of immortality. If we call the words of Scripture upon this topic figurative, — and they could hardly be otherwise, for they who are caught up into the heavens hear what it is neither lawful nor possible to utter, — let us accept the figures, not as exaggerations, but as inadequate, halting, stammering utterances of things too great to be told. If that heavenly city hath "no need of the sun, neither of the moon, to shine in it," it is only because "the glory of God doth lighten it, and the Lamb is the light thereof." If there is "no temple therein," it is only because the "Lord God Almighty and the Lamb are the temple of it." When the senses and the understanding put the old question, "How are the dead raised up, and with what body do they come?" let us hear the great apostle, when he says, "God giveth it a body as it hath pleased him;" and "that which is sown in corruption is raised in incorruption; that which is sown in weakness is raised in power." "We are not so much unclothed as clothed upon: our mortality is swallowed up of life." We want to believe greatly, as Christians should. Like Christian and Hopeful in the immortal "Pilgrim's Progress," we would, sometimes at least, be in heaven before we come to it; "being swallowed up with the sight of angels, and with hearing of their melodious notes." Here also, we are told, "they had the city itself in view; and they thought they heard all the bells therein to ring to welcome them thereto." This world is beautiful, and our Father's; and yet our day of death is a day of emancipation. There is a burden of the flesh. The atmosphere of the earth is laden with heavy and stupefying vapors, and not fit to be the breath of the spirit's life. These bodies are already the temples of the Lord, — marvellous organisms, beautifully fashioned for their place and work. You have all seen how sweetly the light of love will shine from the human face, and how the fruits of wisdom and gentleness will cluster about human lips; and yet it is but an earthen vessel, after all, that guards our treasure. The body is but an imperfect instrument. The mind soon wearies and wears out the brain, the discerning soul overtaxes and exhausts the eye of flesh, and the poor tired limbs totter upon the heart's errand of charity. And then we are limited within, as well as without, — perplexed by mysteries, burdened by infirmities, tempted to fall back from our aspirations and our purposes; and we seem to ourselves like those who move about in sleep, only half conscious of the great realities of our existence. Doubtless there is that in our translation, even when we leave behind the most useful works and the most dearly loved friends, which makes the change most blessed, certainly if we can know that those whom we have left for a short time are at least not sorry as they who have no hope.

I may add, that when the mind is calmed and soothed, if not positively gladdened, by this faith, it is in a condition to consider gratefully how much remains, even when our friend has been taken. The

light of the world into which he has gone is thrown
back upon his earthly life, and adds its own peculiar
charm to what was so beautiful before. If the re-
membrance of the just was blessed, even in the
twilight season of the old religions, how much more
blessed when we know that they have gone from us
to be made perfect! This earth, and all that live
upon it, are seen in their fairest light, only when the
vision of the old patriarch is repeated in our experience, and, before our anointed eyes, a heavenward
path "glows with angel-steps."

You know, my friends, what hath befallen to give
this direction to my thoughts. There is no need that
I should tell you. When the heart of a city is sad-
dened because its light has been withdrawn, its pride
and its joy taken; when the whole land is moved, in
its noisy marts and its quiet retreats, by the tidings of
the death of one who was the nation's boast; when the
world of letters, even beyond the range of our English
speech, deplores and shall deplore the loss of one of
its most faithful and efficient laborers and brightest
ornaments, — we need not pronounce any name; our
minds are irresistibly drawn to contemplate the per-
petual mystery of our living and dying in the light of
our Saviour's everlasting gospel; and we must stay a
moment to gather up the lessons of the earthly days

that have been finished. Moreover, the common bereavement is our special loss and affliction, — how heavily it presses upon one of these households, it would be an intrusion upon the most sacred privacy of grief to tell you; — and although he whose going-out from us we lament was singularly modest and retiring, as eager to escape as too many are to invite the notice of men, it is but fitting, and what even he would pardon, that we should pause upon the meaning of his life, as it comes home to us in this hour. I leave to the brethren of his own noble calling the pleasant task of recording his story, with careful mention of years and months and places. To be so associated with his name will be no slight honor. My concern is not so much with facts of life as with traits of character; not so much with what he did as with what he was. And, even so limited, I must be brief; which I can the better be, since much of what I would have said has already found expression in fitter words than any that I can command, especially by one whose claim to be heard upon a theme so attractive is far stronger than mine. Would that he were the speaker, and I the listener, in this very hour! And yet, for the sake of my subject, I know that you will listen patiently; for he whom we mourn was one whose praises all men loved to hear.

The Christian pulpit has no special concern with

merely intellectual greatness and success. It is
sacred, not secular. It is reared and set apart for
the defence and illustration of the gospel. It is the
preacher's business to set forth spiritual and moral
truth: and, with many whom the world calls great
men, he can have nothing to do, save, perhaps, to
urge that great men are not always wise; or that the
strongest, as well as the feeblest, are alike dependent
upon the great God; or, it may be, with the Christian
apostle and seer, to lift a little the veil which hides
from us the unseen, and show the dead, small and
great, standing before the throne of the Judge. It is
for the world to magnify its own heroes. Let the
dead bury their dead, and pronounce their eulogies.
Here we use wisdom only in that scriptural sense
which includes a distinctively moral element. We
speak only of the truly great and wise; and our word,
even concerning these, touches directly the spiritual
and moral quality of their service and example. And
so my theme is not the scholar, but the Christian
scholar. I speak to you not so much of him, who
with profound and laboriously gained learning, and in
words that charmed at once the wise and the simple,
wrote of the fortunes of men and nations, as of him
who toiled to learn and to tell the truth of man's life,
to paint faithful pictures, and make an honest record
of human experience, — to bring a conscience and a

heart to his high task. It is true, indeed, in a good
sense, as we have learned from the living and dying
and rising of our Lord, that all history is sacred ; that
the hand of God is in it from first to last, and in
Greece, in Italy, in Spain, as well as in Palestine ;
and you will realize yet more, upon a moment's reflec-
tion, how largely the pictures of man's life which our
masterly artist painted illustrate the workings, so
mighty, so instructive, and, as overruled by God, so beneficent, even in their perversions and distortions, of
the ideas which Christ gave to the world. The student of church-history must group about himself such
studies as Ferdinand the Catholic, Philip the Bigot,
Torquemada the Inquisitor, and those terrible con-
querors, half fanatics and half desperadoes, who tried
to forget, in their lust of gold, that God hath given to
us the heathen for our inheritance, not that we may
slay, but that we may convert them. Nevertheless, it
belongs to laborers in the field of literature to record
afresh, as they have so gladly done already, their esti-
mate of the abundant contributions to good learning
made by our great historian. Of the writer, as a
writer, I have only a single word to say here and
now, — one word only, and yet a significant one. I
find a moral quality in our historian's style ; a direct
manifestation therein of the simple integrity of his
soul ; the genuineness and openness of his nature in

his written words; the same transparent clearness upon the page which was to be seen upon the face, — the one, as the other, — a medium which might in no wise hide, but could only reveal, his thought. I cannot but admire a calm, judicial fairness, which would exaggerate nothing for effect, and weighed epithets and adjectives, that are so often regarded as beyond the pale of conscience, as scrupulously as a vulgar honesty weighs gold and merchandise. It is, as I said, no light matter. Words may be written as well as spoken idly: they often are. It is a grave offence to sacrifice truth to rhetoric, fairness and charity to an antithesis, and to be indifferent whether the lights we kindle mislead or no, provided they are only brilliant and fantastic. And it is encouraging to the friend of truth and simplicity to know, that the pure brightness of that honest page found the widest and heartiest appreciation; and that those who would have been wearied and worn out by a false brilliancy found a genuine satisfaction as they yielded themselves to the magic of nature. There is an integrity of intellect as well as of heart. But I need not speak to you of volumes which are in all your dwellings, their contents familiar to your ears as well as your eyes; for the smoothly flowing style encourages audible reading, and makes the books specially welcome to the household circle.

Pass from the writings, then, to the writer. It is not, as is so often the case, an unpleasant transition. What his opponents said of St. Paul is sometimes most unhappily true of the author: "His letters, say they, are weighty and powerful; but his bodily presence is weak, and his speech contemptible." The writings apologize for the man. In this case, had there been any need, it might have been precisely the other way; for, great as the fame of the writer was, it has been truly said that the man was greater. His days were passed, for the most part, in the presence of you all: from boyhood onward, that face of truth and beauty, stamped with such a gentle manliness, has carried about through your streets its unspoken benediction. The friends of his early days, his school and college companions, tell us, that what he has been to us in his last years, just that he was to them in his first years, — that, and no other; as harmless as he was wise, as unassuming as he was gifted; from first to last, genuine and consistent, and a child in malice; neither to be discouraged by difficulty, nor to be spoiled by the abundance of successes and applause. My own personal knowledge of him covers only these few last years; and yet he could not be a stranger. Amongst the pictures of childhood laid up in the mind's image-chamber, there are no portraits more distinct than those of his parents, — honored and beloved both, beyond any common measures. I can see them now, as, on the Lord's Day, they passed quietly and reverently to their seats in our house of worship on yonder Church Green. I can almost fancy that one of them is still wending her way through our streets, in storm as well as in sunshine, none the less a sister of charity because the devoted mother of her own household, — a woman who was the friend at once of the highest and of the lowliest, and who had found not only one sphere, but many. I saw the mother again in the son. And then, on his own part, he would not be a stranger. With a tenderness for the clergyman of his parish, — one of those old-fashioned virtues to which his true conservatism clung, — he was amongst the first in the congregation to seek the pastor, and to welcome him with the word and the look of a friend; and you know what they were from him. And, what he was in the beginning, that he was to the end. More I might say, but may not. It is a privilege to have shared such kindness; but it brings its own sense of bereavement.

This life, which has come to a close for this world, was not without its heroism. I am aware, indeed, that both histories and historian would be likely to make upon the hasty reader and observer the impression of cheaply earned successes. We are ready to say, that what is so easily read must have been easily written; and, where there are no marks of struggle, we conclude that there has been none. But the student knows that easy writing is pretty sure to be hard reading; and the reader of men will tell you, that self-discipline has as much to do as nature in the production of a quiet and genial activity. There was, it is true, a noble being to be unfolded and built upon, — not one talent only, but ten; and yet, in this as in every other case, where any thing really excellent has been achieved, there were obstacles and there was heroism. Think of the patience, the painstaking, and the persistency which could bring so many orderly and reliable and well-told narratives out of a chaos of printed and written volumes, most of them in foreign and even partially obsolete tongues; and this rather with the help of the ear than of the eye. That sadly impaired vision would have been availed of by most young men of fortune as an excuse for an elegant dilettanteism, a graceful trifling, a life of amusement and luxury. But for him it was a sore trial, bravely and sweetly borne; it was a grievous hinderance, stoutly met and triumphed over. The story of the expedients by which the infirmity was in some degree successfully encountered is very touching, and strikingly illustrates the perseverance of a living soul. It is a grand example for those to ponder who fancy

that the parables of the talents are not for them,
because they are not compelled to effort by any stress
of poverty, — for all who accept idleness as their des-
tiny, because others have labored, and they have
entered into their labors.   It is a lesson which is especially valuable in a land where hereditary wealth does
not bring with it, by the very constitution of society,
hereditary duties.   Let our youth weigh it well.
They may not be able to instruct and delight tens of
thousands with their learning and eloquence ; but are
they, therefore, utterly incompetent of good ?   Have
they no errand on the earth, save to eat and drink,
and wear clothes ?   Shall any most frivolous excuse
discharge them from their work ?   In God's name,
let them do something ; let them find each his task,
though it may be a very humble one.   If they can do
nothing else, let them make some wilderness habita-
ble.   The earth is not half subdued ; society is not
half civilized : and we may be sure that the wise
Creator, who himself worketh hitherto, never yet
made an idler.   The very day of his departure found
our friend reproaching himself for an inactivity,
which, to every one else, seemed not only pardonable,
but right, — laying upon weakness tasks which only
strength could bear ; and, when the angel of God
came to summon him, the materials and the instru-
ments of his life-long industry were awaiting his

hand; and he died, as he had lived, a worker. De-
scribing once a chronic difficulty of vision, — a mote
thrusting itself for ever into the line of light, — he
said, very quietly, " I presume, that, if it were flitting
before your eyes, you would not be inclined to use
them at all: I have become accustomed to it." Patience had its perfect work, — so perfect, that she
made no sign.

But the greatest charm has as yet only been hinted
at. I find an intellect obedient to the man, and not
a man subordinated to an intellect. It is the vice of
the intellect to usurp the domain of the whole being.
Hence the conceit of knowledge and the foolishness
of wisdom; hence arrogance, jealousies, rivalries, evil
speakings, magisterial airs, and intellectual despotisms.
Let a man become a mere intellect, and he is intolera-
ble; and all his learning will win for him no loyalty
of admiration and affection. We grow weary of the
pedant; and, when he is gone, we do not desire him.
One, who knew our friend more thoroughly than
any, has told me that he did not seem to care much for
intellect, or to exact learning and the like from others.
It was, simply, that he cared so much more for our
large and various humanity, as it makes the home
blessed and beautiful; as it is displayed in childhood,
youth, and age; as it is seen in common, every-day
conditions: it was, simply, that he was a true demo-

crat, without any demagogic ways and airs; and a true philanthropist, though he never compassed sea and land to the neglect of the nearest and dearest. I think the human face was dear to him. He could not let you go by him in the street, without exchanging a word as well as a sign of greeting, — a word that was sure to be as cheerful as his look, and to witness unconsciously for his loving nature. He did not love men because he was blind to their faults; but he was blind to the faults of men because he loved them. It was this abundance of love that made his character so gentle and almost womanly; for his was the might of gentleness. Perhaps, as our poor humanity must always purchase its successes at a price, this incapacity to dwell upon faults amounted almost to a defect. Certainly, if there be any merit in being a good hater, it was a merit to which he could lay no claim.

Of the interior life, I have no report to make to you. I think that he was chary of speech upon directly religious subjects; preferring to witness for his convictions by works rather than by words, and, in an age which is afflicted with much confused and insignificant and aimless discussion of the deepest themes, choosing the refuge of silence. That he prized the worship of the church, I know; that his spirit was profoundly reverent, and his allegiance to

the truth unhesitating, I am more than satisfied. I
rejoice that he can never be confounded with those
men of letters, so numerous, alas! in our day, who
openly neglect or affect to patronize the gospel.
I know that he loved the Lord's house, and that such
of its forms as he saw his way clear to accept were
for him no formalities. More I cannot tell you. If
you would judge the heart, see what flowed out from
its abundance.

Do you ask me, Had he no faults? I answer,
Undoubtedly; for he was human : and yet, as I do not
know what they were, I cannot tell you of them if I
would.

But my memorial must be brought to an end. It
is a poor picture; but, for that, you must blame not
the subject, but the artist. My friends, it was sad to
know, as we rose up in our sanctuary about our
honored dead on that day of weeping, that we should
see him no more on this earth for ever; that we
should seek for him in vain in his accustomed seat in
this house of prayer : but sadness shall give place
to cheerful hope, at least to resignation and trust, if
we will be Christians in very deed as in name. So
may God consecrate this grief to the nearest and to
the more removed! It hath been resurrection-time,
you know, since our Lord went to the Father. The
memorials that are spread out before us to-day re-

mind us of a victory as well as of a defeat: for He who died for our sins, rose for our justification; and the gospel that is preached unto you is a word of life and immortality.